W9-BNC-485

RYE FREE READING ROOM

TOMIE dePAOLA

Strega Nona
DOES IT AGAIN

NANCY PAULSEN BOOKS ✿ AN IMPRINT OF PENGUIN GROUP (USA) INC.

DEPAOLA

To my entire Italian family, especially those in Paris!

And to Bernadette Peters,
whose inspiring hair is only outdone by her remarkable voice and talent.
I love you, and "Angelina" does too.

NANCY PAULSEN BOOKS
An imprint of Penguin Young Readers Group
Published by The Penguin Group
Penguin Group (USA) Inc., 375 Hudson Street, New York, NY 10014, USA

USA | Canada | UK | Ireland | Australia | New Zealand | India | South Africa | China
Penguin Books Ltd, Registered Offices: 80 Strand, London WC2R 0RL, England
For more information about the Penguin Group, visit penguin.com

Copyright © 2013 by Tomie dePaola.
All rights reserved. No part of this book may be reproduced, scanned or distributed in any printed or electronic form without permission
in writing from the publisher. Nancy Paulsen Books, Reg. U.S. Pat. & Tm. Off. Please do not participate in or encourage
piracy of copyrighted materials in violation of the author's rights. Purchase only authorized editions.

Library of Congress Cataloging-in-Publication Data
DePaola, Tomie, 1934– author, illustrator.
Strega Nona does it again / Tomie dePaola.
pages cm
Summary: Strega Nona has the perfect remedy for a houseguest who overstays her welcome.
[1. Witches—Fiction.] I. Title.   PZ7.D439Spm 2013   [E]—dc23   2012048224

Published simultaneously in Canada.
Manufactured in China by South China Printing Co. Ltd.
ISBN 978-0-399-25781-0
1 3 5 7 9 10 8 6 4 2

Design by Marikka Tamura.
Text set in Golden Cockerel ITC Std.
The art was done in acrylics on Arches 180 lb. handmade watercolor paper.
The publisher does not have any control over and does not assume any responsibility for author
or third-party websites or their content.

Dear Cousin Strega Nona,

As you know, our oldest daughter,
Angelina, has grown into quite a beauty, which
is wonderful and terrible all at once.

All the young men of the town are chasing after her. Every
night, they keep the whole household awake while they sing love
songs. They leave so many flowers and gifts at the gate we can
hardly get in or out. They are a general nuisance.

All except Hugo, the son of Duke Fabio. Angelina claims she
is in love with him, but he doesn't seem to notice. He's always
looking at himself in the mirror. Angelina is very
unhappy. My wife and I think the only solution is for her
to leave our village until she forgets Hugo.

Would you mind if she stayed with you? She can arrive
in a few days.

Grazie, thank you, dear cousin.
Duke Andrea di Limone and his wife

P.S. I want to warn you that Angelina is a "handful."

"Well," said Strega Nona to Big Anthony and Bambolona, "it looks like we're going to have a visitor—my cousin's daughter is coming.

It will be nice for you two to have some company your age. I'll give Angelina my bedroom and sleep on the bed in the kitchen. Now let's get ready."

"Here she comes, Strega Nona!" said Big Anthony.

"*Benvenuto,* Angelina, welcome."

"*Povero mei,* dear me!" Strega Nona said softly. "So much luggage!"

"Big Anthony, help unload the cart," Strega Nona said.

"And Bambolona, please show Angelina her room."

Angelina was not an easy guest.

"I don't like this room! My room at home is blue with pink flowers."

"I don't eat pasta. At home I eat fresh fruit!"

"I need a maid. At home I have a maid. Bambolona, you can be my maid!"

"I've never been a maid. What does a maid do?" asked Bambolona.

"First of all, she wears a uniform. And she does *everything*
I tell her to do!"

"I need a footman. At home I have a footman," Angelina said.
"Big Anthony, you can be my footman."
"What's a footman?" asked Big Anthony.

"Well, my footman will wait on me, open the door for me,
run errands, and help Bambolona to do everything I tell you.
And," Angelina said with a big smile, "you'll get to wear a
beautiful uniform—just like Bambolona."

Angelina called Big Anthony and Bambolona to her. "I have this picture of my love, Hugo. Let's make a shrine for it. After all, we are both the fairest of them all. Gather branches, flowers, anything to make it pretty."

"It's beautiful," Angelina said. "Now, let's take a stroll. Footman, you will hold my *ombrellino*—parasol. Maid, you will walk ahead of me carrying a basket full of flowers. You will scatter petals so I can walk on them instead of the dirty path."

"*Ragazzo*—boy," Angelina called to a child who was playing. "Run ahead to town and tell everyone that Angelina, daughter of Duke Andrea di Limone, will honor them with a visit today, so they should prepare to meet me!"

Back at home, Strega Nona was looking for Big Anthony and Bambolona.

"Where did those two go?" she asked herself.

"Oh, well, I'll just have to do their chores myself."

"*Povero mei*—dear me!" Strega Nona said when she saw Angelina's room. "What happened here?"

Then Strega Nona spied the shrine. "Well, I'll have to do something about all this."

Meanwhile, back in town, Angelina waved to the crowd.
"*Arrivederci, tutti*—good-bye, all! Don't be sad, I'll try to return!"

"Who does she think she is?" the mayor's wife said.
"I hope she *never* comes back!"

Later that night, Big Anthony and Bambolona went to see Strega Nona.
"How much longer is she going to stay?" Big Anthony asked. "She keeps me
so busy that I don't have time to do my chores."

"Me too," chimed in Bambolona. "She has me running around like
a crazy chicken. And it's 'maid this, maid that'! And you should have
seen her in town. She bossed everyone around—even the mayor and
the sisters of the convent."

"Don't worry, my children," Strega Nona said. "I have a plan."

"Angelina," called Strega Nona, "can you come and join me by your shrine?"

"So," said Strega Nona, "it looks like you care a lot for Hugo."

"Oh, I do, Strega Nona. But he doesn't even know he deserves me," Angelina complained.

"Well, maybe *we* can help!" said Strega Nona, holding up the magic book. "In here is a spell for a potion for young ladies who want husbands! And I have another idea. Because Hugo likes to look at himself so much, why not change the picture in your shrine with a mirror!"

"Oh, Strega Nona, yes, yes, yes!" cried Angelina.
"But you must be patient, my dear. Let's see what happens."

That night, Strega Nona wrote a letter to Duke Andrea.

·Dear· Cousin· Andrea;
·I· think· I· have· the· solution· for· your· "problem."
·Please· come· to· fetch· Angelina;
·but· be· sure· to· bring· along· Hugo—
·at· any· cost.· I· don't· care· how· you·
·manage· it—just· do· it:

    ·Amore· e· baci—love· and· Kisses;
·Your· Cousin; Strega· Nona.

A few days later, a letter arrived. "Angelina, your father is coming to take you home," Strega Nona said. "And guess what. Hugo is with him!"

"Now, Angelina," Strega Nona whispered. "Here is the special potion. The minute Hugo sees the shrine, drink it."
"What will happen?" Angelina asked.
"You'll see," said Strega Nona.

Hugo fell in love with the shrine immediately. "How beautiful!" he said, staring at himself. "You really understand me!"

"We understand each other," Angelina said.

"Will you marry me?" Hugo asked.

"Yes, yes, yes!" shouted Angelina. "I thought you'd never ask!"

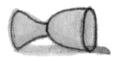

"*Arrivederci*—good-bye. Safe journey and best wishes for a happy wedding," everyone called out as the carts were leaving.

"Boy, is he going to be busy!" said Big Anthony.

"So is she!" said Bambolona.

"They deserve each other," Strega Nona said.

"How did you know?" Big Anthony and Bambolona asked.

"Aha, the magic of mirrors!" said Strega Nona. "They were both in love . . ."

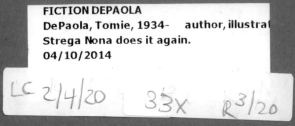

FICTION DEPAOLA
DePaola, Tomie, 1934-   author, illustrat
Strega Nona does it again.
04/10/2014

LC 2/4/20   33x   R³/20